The Adventures of Quint The Bookmobile

The Big Move To RoneyVille

By Kathleen Quinton
Illustrated by Eminence System

Quintessential Productions
Marlborough, Massachusetts, USA

Inspired by the Quints everywhere who bravely come forward to share their own special brand of magic. Thank you for making our world a better place.

Acknowledgements:

Editor: Kim Carr

Illustrators: Eminence System

Published by Quintessential Productions,

Marlborough, Massachusetts, United States of America

Library of Congress Control Number: 2018956354

Publisher's Cataloging-In-Publication Data

(Prepared by The Donohue Group, Inc.)

Names: Quinton, Kathleen, author. | Eminence System, illustrator.

Title: The adventures of Quint the Bookmobile. [Book 1], The big move to Roneyville / by Kathleen Quinton ; illustrated by Eminence System.

Other Titles: Big move to Roneyville

Description: Marlborough, Massachusetts, USA : Quintessential Productions, [2018] | Interest age level: 004-008. | Summary: "Quint the Bookmobile moves from his home at the big red shop to join Ms. Morris, the librarian, at his new home, the Tremell Library in Roneyville. An interactive book with hidden keys to find."--Provided by publisher.

Identifiers: ISBN 9781513636115 (hardcover) | ISBN 9781513636122 (softcover) | ISBN 9781513636139 (Kindle)

Subjects: LCSH: Bookmobiles--Juvenile fiction. | Moving, Household--Juvenile fiction. | Libraries--Juvenile fiction. | CYAC: Bookmobiles--Fiction. | Moving, Household--Fiction. | Libraries--Fiction.
Classification: LCC PZ7.1.Q65 Ad 2018 (print) | LCC PZ7.1.Q65 (ebook) | DDC [E]--dc23

To the Reader:

When I was small, a big bookmobile would park down the street from my house. Bookmobile day was one of my favorite days of the week. All the neighborhood kids would visit the bookmobile at the same time. We would search through the shelves hoping to borrow the most magical book ever! If we had a book report due or needed to brush up on a certain subject, the bookmobile librarians were on the case! It was a time of innocence and fun, and books were for everyone.

Bookmobiles have come a long way since they were invented. Have you ever visited a traveling library? In some places in the world, traveling libraries arrive

by bicycle...
by boat...
by camel...
by donkey...
or even by elephant!
Come, let's meet a present-day bookmobile.

It is the day of the big move! Quint the Bookmobile is leaving the three generations of shopkeepers and the hustle and bustle of the big red shop where he came to life.

(Shhh... don't tell! And be on the lookout for some hidden keys on this adventure, too!)

Quint's favorite part of living in the big red shop is when Joe the friendly mail carrier comes by and gives Quint's best buddy Barnabus a bone each day. It's always SO much fun to watch Barnabus go crazy waiting for his bone!

In the nearby town of Roneyville, Ms. Morris the librarian reads books to children every day in the Tremell Library. She loves how stories spark imaginations and hold the keys to so much knowledge. The library's motto is "BOOKS! BOOKS ARE FOR EVERYONE, WHEREVER THEY MAY BE!"

TREMELL LIBRARY

Today, Ms. Morris is happily waiting in the parking lot of the big red shop to bring Quint on his first adventure. She is SO excited! Quint is filled with over 4,000 books!

Can you imagine 4,000 books?! And now with the ready-to-travel Quint, Tremell Library really can get books to everyone, wherever they may be!

Time to go! Quint gulps, gathers up his courage and puffs out his hood in pride. Bob the shop manager opens the huge red garage door. Quint winks goodbye to his best friend Barnabus the big brown dog and pulls slowly forward.

“First stop, town square!” Ms. Morris exclaims. Bring on the hilly streets of Roneyville! Quint thinks, “Oh, I hope the townspeople will like me!” He bravely faces his fear with his headlights on.

I think I am ready...
I hope I am ready...
I am ready!

Quint knows he has a mission to fulfill.
Roneyville, get ready. Here we come!

QUINT

As they round the last curve, they see the town square. Men, women, and children have lined the streets. Ms. Morris and Quint spy balloons and streamers decorating the square. Quint is excited to see that so many people came to meet him. Ms. Morris pulls the lovable bookmobile to a stop.

QUINT
Quint sees the three generations of shopkeepers from the big red shop. Wow, they even brought Barnabus the big brown dog with them, too. He is running around in circles and wagging his tail wildly!

One by one, the townspeople explore their new Tremell Library bookmobile.

Quint is no longer afraid that they won't like him. He thinks to himself, "They love me!"

Ms. Morris is over the moon, too! She knows what sharing the keys of knowledge will mean to the town.

Finally, Barnabus the big brown dog stops running around in circles. He sits right down next to the oldest of the three shopkeepers, who pats him on the head.
Then the shopkeeper winks directly at Quint.

Quint smiles wide and gives them both a wink of
his own. He puffs out his hood with pride.
Quint's first mission is complete.

Ms. Morris must be tired from all the excitement. Did she really see Quint wink at the shopkeepers? No, that's just plain silly!

On to the next adventure...

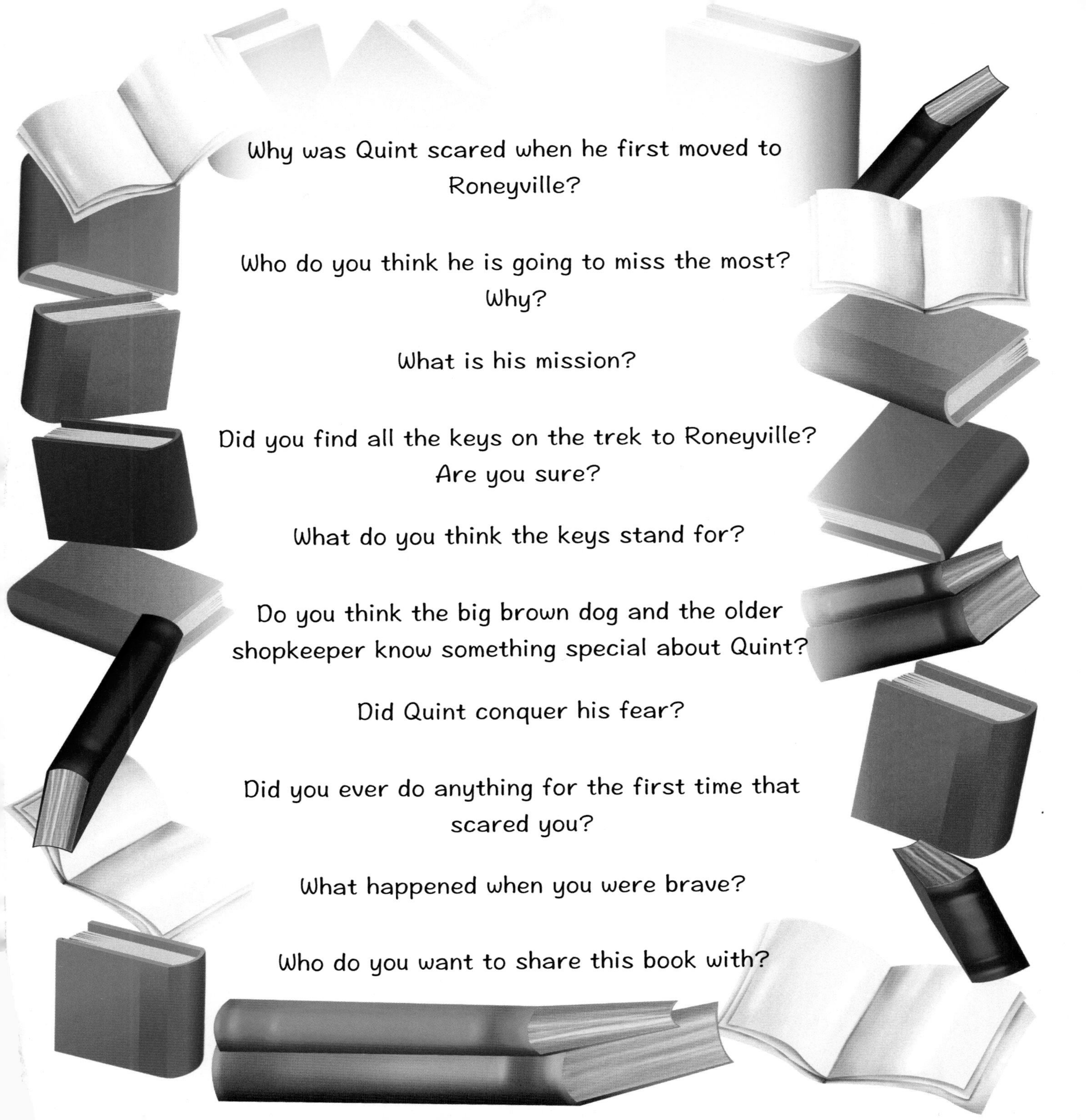

Why was Quint scared when he first moved to Roneyville?

Who do you think he is going to miss the most? Why?

What is his mission?

Did you find all the keys on the trek to Roneyville? Are you sure?

What do you think the keys stand for?

Do you think the big brown dog and the older shopkeeper know something special about Quint?

Did Quint conquer his fear?

Did you ever do anything for the first time that scared you?

What happened when you were brave?

Who do you want to share this book with?

68525965R00015

Made in the USA
Columbia, SC
08 August 2019